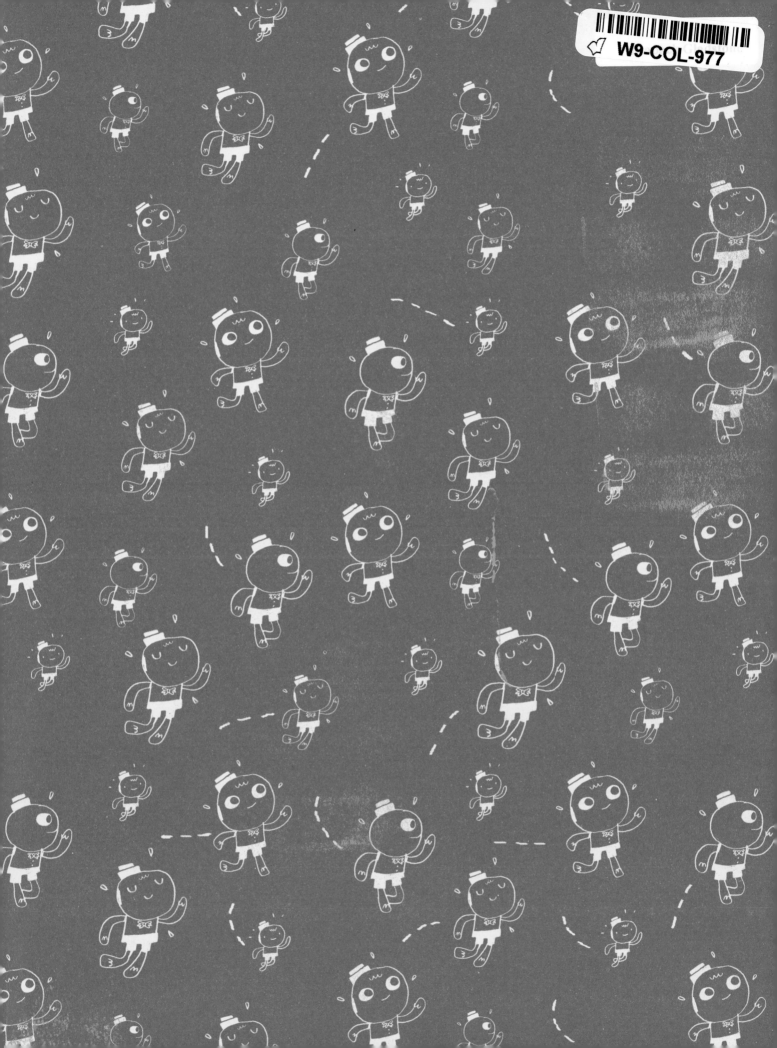

To my mom, Shirley, and my dad, Doug—
So much of who I am and what I strive to be
is a reflection of your love, encouragement, and guidance.
Thank you! With love, your youngest crumb-snatcher.

And a special thanks to the Fairfax County Fire and Rescue
Station # 1, McLean, Virginia—for your outstanding service
to our community, and your enthusiastic help
as I researched details of this book.
—L.M.

To my most favorit-est people
in the whole wide world:
Katrin and Allister.
—M.L.

G. P. PUTNAM'S SONS A division of Penguin Young Readers Group.
Published by The Penguin Group. Penguin Group (USA) Inc., 375 Hudson Street, New York, NY 10014,
U.S.A. Penguin Group (Canada), 90 Eglinton Avenue East, Suite 700, Toronto, Ontario M4P 2Y3, Canada
(a division of Pearson Penguin Canada Inc.). Penguin Books Ltd, 80 Strand, London WC2R ORL, England.
Penguin Ireland, 25 St. Stephen's Green, Dublin 2, Ireland (a division of Penguin Books Ltd). Penguin
Group (Australia), 250 Camberwell Road, Camberwell, Victoria 3124, Australia (a division of Pearson
Australia Group Pty Ltd). Penguin Books India Pvt Ltd, 11 Community Centre, Panchsheel Park, New
Delhi - 110 017, India. Penguin Group (NZ), 67 Apollo Drive, Rosedale, Auckland 0632, New Zealand
(a division of Pearson New Zealand Ltd). Penguin Books South Africa, Rosebank Office Park, 181 Jan
Smuts Avenue, Parktown North 2193, South Africa. Penguin China, B7 Jiaming Center, 27 East Third
Ring Road North, Chaoyang District, Beijing 100020, China. Penguin Books Ltd, Registered Offices:
80 Strand, London WC2R ORL, England.

Text copyright © 2013 by Laura Murray. Illustrations copyright © 2013 by Mike Lowery.

Published simultaneously in Canada. Manufactured in China by South China Printing Co. Ltd.
Design by Ryan Thomann. Text set in Bokka and Dr. Eric, with a bit of hand-lettering.
The illustrations were rendered with pencil, traditional screen printing, and digital color.

Library of Congress Cataloging-in-Publication Data
Murray, Laura, 1970- The Gingerbread Man loose on the fire truck / Laura Murray ; illustrated
by Mike Lowery. p. cm. Summary: When the Gingerbread Man joins the children who made him on a
school field trip to a fire station, he escapes being eaten by Spot the Dalmatian and rides along
to a fire. [1. Stories in rhyme. 2. Cookies—Fiction. 3. Fire departments—Fiction. 4. School field
trips—Fiction.] I. Lowery, Mike, 1980- ill. II. Title. PZ8.3.M9368Gjf 2013 [E]—dc23 2012029867
ISBN 978-0-399-25779-7 / 10 9 8 7 6 5 4 3 2 1

The pocket was cozy.
I peeked from the **top**.

The **bus** drove for miles,
then came to a **stop**.

In front of a building with shiny red **doors**
stood two **firefighters** from **Company Four**.

One had on **gear** for a quick **demonstration,**
and standing beside him was **Spot,** the **Dalmatian.**

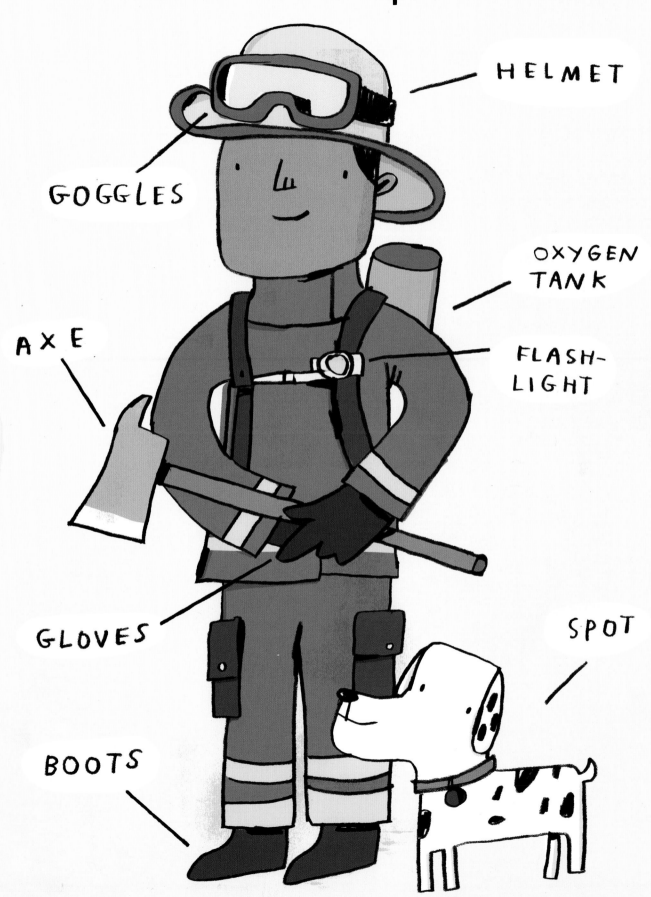

HELMET

GOGGLES

OXYGEN
TANK

AXE

FLASH-
LIGHT

GLOVES

SPOT

BOOTS

I was **jOStled** and **jiggled** as kids moved about. Then **I** fell from the **pocket,**

right on the **DOG'S SNOUT!**

spot sniffed at my face, taking one sticky **lick**.

I needed a **TRICK** to get out of there **QUICK!**

He **tossed** me up high with his mouth open **wide**,

but I **flipped** toward his tail and slid down, like a **slide**.

My feet hit the **ground**. I took off for the **station**,

but right on my **heels** was that hungry **Dalmatian**.

The class didn't notice. They tried on black **boots,**

and helmets, and air tanks, and big heavy suits.

I dashed to the **fire truck**,
jumped in a **Seat**.

I **hopped** on the steering wheel, gave it a **spin—** and yelled out

HONK HONK!

with a big cookie **grin.**

The **wheel** spun past **gauges** and **switches** and **knobs—** and all kinds of **buttons** that do different **jobs.**

Then I heard someone whistle.
Spot trotted away,

So I jumped through the window without a delay.

I landed on top of a big silver bowl.

OH NO!
I cried out
as I leapt for a pole.

SPOT

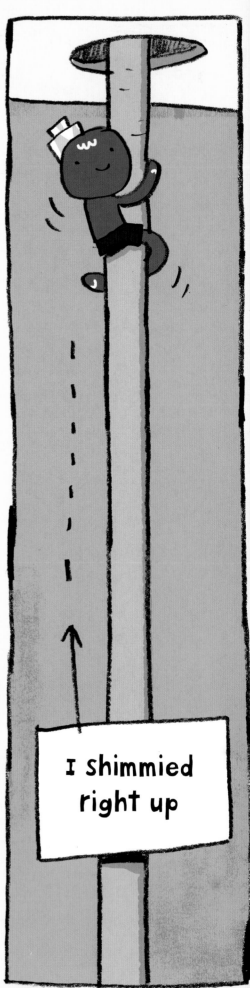

I shimmied right up

and I **sprang** from the **top**, then jumped on a bed

with a big **BELLY FLOP.**

There were several more bunks with their covers pulled **tight** for each **firefighter** who stayed through the **night.**

I **bounced** on each bed on my way to the **door**, then into a room with a bright checkered **floor.**

I peeked 'round the **corner** and smelled something **yummy**—

a grumbling sound **rumbled** up from my **tummy**.

I **spotted** a fireman filling up bowls with **five-alarm chili** and buttery **rolls**.

Then all of a sudden, I heard a loud noise.

WOOOOo

FIRE!

one shouted.

NO LUNCH FOR US, BOYS . . .

They rushed to the

BUNK ROOM

and slid down the

POLE.

I followed behind them, then peered down the hole.

Spot wasn't there—
a **sure** sign of **good** luck.
So I slipped down the pole
and then **jumped** on the **truck**.

I'LL **RIDE** TO THE **RESCUE**,
AS FAST AS I CAN.
I WANT TO HELP, TOO! I'M THE
GINGERBREAD MAN!

WHEEE - EEEEE

went the **sirens**. The lights flashed **around**

as I **zoomed**
past my classmates,
below on the **ground**.

We sped through the streets and I clung to the back,

near **ladders** and **hoses** piled up in a **stack**.

The **engine** pulled up. Firefighters jumped **out**.
They rushed to the **hydrant** and opened the **spout**.

I spied a large house with a **shed** near the **back**.
Smoke rose from its window, all sooty and **black**.

I grabbed the hose nozzle and gave it a **pull**,

but that hose whipped and bucked like a rodeo **bull**.

The water **whooshed** out and it doused the old **shed**, and the powerful spray shot the hat off my **head**.

The chief ran up quickly and dove on the hose.

She crawled her way up till we came nose to nose.

LOOK, EVERYONE! IT'S A GINGERBREAD MAN. NOW, WHERE DID YOU COME FROM?

said Fire Chief Anne.

I CAME WITH THE CHILDREN TO VISIT THE STATION. BUT I ALMOST GOT EATEN BY SPOT, THE DALMATIAN!

We packed up the **truck** and drove back to the **station**.
We pulled in the drive to a standing **ovation**.

The children **applauded** and shouted out **"YAY!"**
They held me up **high**, yelling,

YOU SAVED THE DAY!

YOU'RE REALLY A HERO!
YOU'RE PART OF OUR CREW,
BUT YOU'RE MISSING YOUR HAT,
SO WE HAVE ONE FOR YOU.

"A SHINY RED **HELMET**
FROM COMPANY FOUR!

THERE ARE MORE FOR
YOUR **CLASSMATES**
STACKED UP BY **THE DOOR.**"

I tried on my helmet and shouted,

WOO-HOO! I'M A GINGERBREAD MAN AND A FIREMAN, TOO!

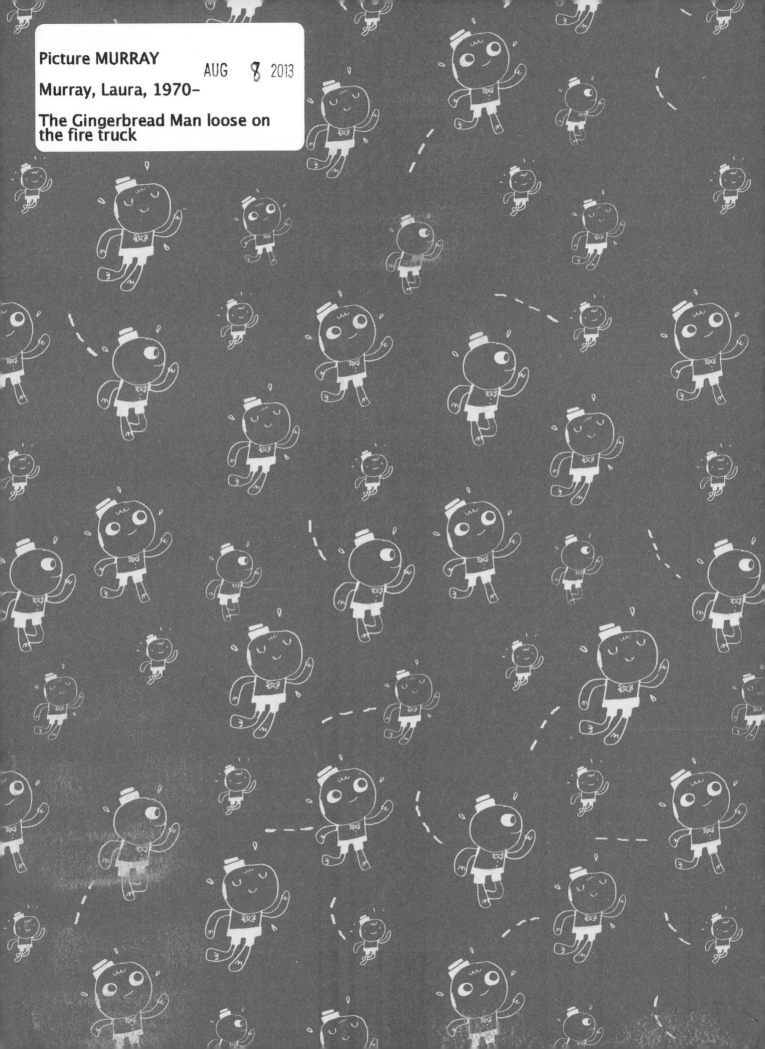